T0193294

INTERNALLY MISPLACED
By Wambui Mwangi

KWANINI? SERIES
is published by Kwani Trust
P.O. Box 2895 00100,
Nairobi, Kenya
Tel: +254 020 235 7295/ 374 5210

E-mail: info@kwani.org

ISBN: 9966-7008-8-9

Cover illustration: Black Butterfly Limited
Design and layout: Sokoletu Creative Limited

Kwani Trust
is a Ford Foundation grantee

www.kwani.org

Internally Misplaced

DESPITE HIS ANXIETY, Margaret Dorobo's driver, Seth Karanja, is in a philosophical mood as he swings left off Ngong Road onto Elgeyo Marakwet. He is very tired, and resigned to it, because he expects fear to continue to keep him awake.

It is one of those warm days in Nairobi, beautiful and sunny, where from some angles, the light seems silver, and many drivers have their windows rolled down.

He checks the rearview mirror again. Nairobi traffic is an exponentially-calculated product of the state of Nairobi's roads. As he eases around a large pothole, the box in the boot of the car shifts slightly, but there is no time to stop and secure it. The potholes are almost alive, he thinks, in the way they grow. The jagged holes give birth to rounded but deeper adolescents, gradually develop into self-conscious trenches, and finally join together to become one full-fledged adult abyss.

A woman drives past: she is wearing a red top with thin straps drooping over her shoulders, and a baseball cap with "Yankees" written on it. Seth marks the angle of her cheekbone, the crease of her eye, the slope of her nostrils—something about the set of her lips reminds him of his niece, Wacera. She is probably one of us, he thinks. Or maybe not; it is so difficult to know, these days.

Seth's secret favourite book of the Bible is the Song of Solomon. He enjoys, with a satisfying mixture of shame and virtuous diligence, all the talk of doe-eyed women and of pomegranate breasts, of dripping myrrh and of the stirring passion of the beloved's caress.

Madam is not in the car today, so Seth allows himself to pick his nose. His thoughts follow his finger around his nostrils, enjoying the voluptuous feel of stretching and probing the spongy inner surfaces. If pushed to it, he could explain why it is acceptable to

6

pick his nose in front of his mother, but not in front of Madam, or why it is possible to pick his nose in Madam's car but never in Madam's house. He is sure that all behaviours have geographies and economies, that they have their own proper places and times, and that the wiping of foreheads, picking of noses, scratching of buttocks, cleaning of ears, or picking of teeth are actions to be indulged in only outside of the territory of his employer's gaze.

The order of eating and drinking in Madam's house is that Madam's Husband can have anything he wants. Madam can have anything Madam's Husband does not want. Then first the indoors staff (drivers first, although they work outside), and then the outdoors staff can have anything after that, if it is already open or in use and at least half-way consumed, and is not a specialty item like butter or Ribena or rice, and of course nothing like Madam's yoghurt – although wine has been subverted by Joshua into the exception to this rule – but if there are guests then they move to the top of the list, even above Madam's Husband.

The guests of Madam or of Madam's Husband can have anything they want, at anytime, full time, anything at all, at all times. This is a rule of the house. Never question guests, never contradict them, never embarrass them, never see or hear anything that might cause them discomfort of any kind: this was hospitality of the old-fashioned and now-rare Kikuyu kind. Unless Madam's Husband asks you about the guest, and then you must remember everything, and you must repeat it in good language and clear speech, no stammering or hesitating or scratching your head, and then never bring it up again: but this happens only rarely.

With all the other worries he has, Seth muses, if he had been a drinking man he would have been an alcoholic by now: like Joshua, the cook at Madam's house, who has an elaborate relationship with Madam's liquor cabinet. Joshua is happiest when either cooking an unpronounceable European meal, or providing Saturday afternoon refreshments for Madam's women friends. This is not because of any pressing gourmet reasons or dictates of hospitality, but because in the first case, Joshua can demand wine for all his recipes, and in the second case, Madam's friends always ask for white wine. These sorts of occasions leave Joshua multiple opportunities for the covert slaking of his sadly expensive thirst. Unfortunately for Joshua, Madam's Husband most often asks for meals consisting of such components as ugali or githeri, and, even worse, Madam herself rarely entertains.

Internally Misplaced

Sometimes, though, especially after he had consumed most of the liquid ingredients and all of the liquid leftovers of an especially French dinner, Joshua could be induced to break into weaving performances of iskuti, to which he would accompany himself by voice. Joshua had trained at Utalii College. He mentions this at least twice a week, as if it had been America or something, as if he had been rich and powerful there, but in any case Utalii is where he acquired his imprudent but powerful taste for wine. Between Joshua's Utalii memories and Madam's generosity, there are never any unfinished boxes of South African wine in Madam's house. Nothing left over; everything put to use, and eaten or drank.

Familiar amusement at Joshua's frailties is almost but not quite enough to lighten the dread weighing Seth's bowels down like a stone. The terrible conversation he had with Jackson this morning is now rancid in his mind. It had been very strange because Jackson, although always indefinably menacing, is usually very silent and polite. He intimidates mostly by withholding himself, so Seth had not known that Jackson had these thoughts brewing in his head. Usually, trying to read Jackson's thoughts is like trying to see the occupant of a car with tinted windows. You simply cannot tell, without a lot of strenuous effort, what is in there—it might be anyone at all.

This morning, Seth had only been cracking a Luo joke, but Jackson's surprisingly long answer had been as serious as his face. He had spoken with a flat passion worn drab and tattered at its edges. Seth had not really seen Jackson before—never really looked so as to see properly, putting effort into his vision, making his eyes strain to see deeper. What he had seen this morning had made his heart burrow deeper into his chest like a small creature hiding away from a sudden light.

Jackson definitely frightens Seth more than Madam's Husband. Madam's Husband is a very soft-spoken man; he orders his world through a whisper. He murmurs into the air, at no-one at all, and things mysteriously happen to his satisfaction, or else. Seth does not know, and never wants to know, or else what.

Yet, while Seth considers Madam's Husband a sort of major shareholder in the universe, one of those men who is sometimes obliged to share his castoffs, but never to divulge or explain his acts, he himself experiences Madam's Husband as an impending disastrous event, like a potential flood or a threatened famine, which requires a soothsayer to avert. Mundu

10

mugo. Exactly. Luckily, Madam's Husband does not often speak to Seth, and Jackson does not often speak to anyone at all.

***

Jackson is madam's Husband's driver. He is a very tall and white gap-toothed compatriot from the lakeside region. Seth thinks of Luos in these elliptical turns because his fastidious mind prefers the scenic route, and also because he knows the power of names to summon daemons, and he is afraid. Jackson is only below Madam's husband in the domestic hierarchy. Jackson is tops, even more than Muthee. Muthee is so old, he really can't do much anymore, although he pretends to: laboriously moving brooms from one end of the house to another, and mops and buckets as well. He has his own broom, mop and bucket for this purpose; nobody else uses them, and if they go missing he gets terribly upset.

Jackson is really the main guy, the one who goes everywhere Madam's Husband goes. He has heard the business deals in the back of the car, he knows what's what, the big bucks, the payload. Jackson would have known which minister was getting fired, when; he knows what arrangements have been made. But does he say? Never.

Jackson has two cell phones. One line is just for Madam's Husband's use, direct; only he can call that line and it has to be answered at once, at any time of the day or night, answered after only one ring, or else. Seth has heard Jackson answer Madam's Husbands phone calls many times at night from the bedroom next door. Jackson says "Yes, Sir," once, like that, as soon as he answers the phone, then he listens and says "Yes, Sir" again, and hangs up. That's all: two words, two times. Yes Sir and Yes Sir. Then Jackson hangs up, picks up the car keys, and leaves. He never reveals where he is going or, on his return, what he has seen. Jackson is always preoccupied, always absorbed in matters that he cannot and will not discuss.

Look where Anastasia's female foolishness had landed her now. Seth shrugs his shoulders, but instantly feels irresponsible. He should do something, but then again, what can he do? She is not the first girl to whom this has happened, although it is unfortunate that it has happened to his niece. Seth knows that the matter of his niece will soon require decisive action from him, and the knowledge fills him with a resentful but unfocused anger.

He fingers the knot of his uniform tie with one hand

and tightens the cloth at his neck. At that moment, one of those pedestrians with a near-mystic faith in the driving skills of Nairobi drivers hurls himself jauntily into the road almost under Seth's wheels, causing Seth to tap the brakes sharply, rebukingly, once, and then gently once more to an abrupt but still-controlled stop. The pedestrian looks at him in calm surprise, as if possible dreadful injury to himself were a new idea. Seth wants to weep at his innocence, but a half second later, he is angry: who is this foolish boy who can still look like that in Nairobi after everything that has happened? Did he just land at JKIA today? It will not take him long to get that Jackson look in his eye. Yes, Seth thinks, if he was a drinking man, he would certainly have been an alcoholic twice over by now. In these times, only the mad can be said to be truly sane.

Seth slows down at the junction of Elgeyo Marakwet and Argwings Khodek, indicates right, and seeing a promising gap between a black Audi and a black Toyota Starlet—one of those cars that Madam's friends' children seem to like - swings the green Mercedes into the lane of traffic on Argwings Khodek with a dignified haste. The treacle-line of cars moves in imperceptible inches forward, then suddenly speeds up for no reason at all, hiccups, and steadies out. Seth sighs as he upshifts hopefully and then morosely downshifts again. He slows down for a speed bump. There is a white Toyota Corolla behind him, and even before Seth has finished slowing down to negotiate the bump, the driver of the Corolla, a fat man in an unwisely- patterned orange shirt, is hooting impatiently at Seth to start moving faster. Seth waits two heartbeats before engaging first gear. He is that sort of person.

He never offers his hand first for shaking.

The man in the Corolla behind him hoots again, short sharp prods of sound which Seth largely ignores. As far as Seth is concerned, Nairobi drivers are always in a rush to get to unimportant places. They always behave as if at their destination there are lives waiting to be saved. The man in the orange shirt is in a hurry to buy a kilo of beef, Seth thinks, which this man will take to his wife, like a dog offering a dead rat to its owner, only to find that she has decided to cook chicken that day, and is anyway having an affair with the neighbour. Humph. People who think vast haste implies a matching importance.

Seth lets the turning signal noise click on and off three times at least, before turning the wheel. He understands that true importance lies in making people wait; in being able to move slowly and in knowing that you can retard all emotions to your speed. Rushing around implies a serious loss of control of your world.

***

A matatu blares past on the right, having edged out oncoming traffic. It elbows past him like a rugby player with the goal posts in sight, driving on the wrong side of the road, intimidating other drivers into collusion with it, and leaving, along with a cloud of diesel smoke, a faint suggestion of a defiant bass rhythm in its wake. Seth notes that the back left-hand corner of the matatu has a broken tail-light. A coil of panic slithers into Seth's belly. He belches deliberately, for distraction, and adjusts his hands on the wheel, his knuckles tight.

Seth's hands are set in the ten-to-two position on the wheel. They are chapped and the approximate shade of grey-brown of the bark of a certain kind of Jacaranda tree that lines Waiyaki Way. It is a colour that speaks of complicated lives, like the ones Nairobi jacaranda trees have had—troubled by blight and inattention, influenced in unnamed ways by forgotten white rulers, rescued for political reasons from being pulled out, like good molars threatened by a greedy dentist, then neglected again: an intermittent nurturing that has left them strangely resilient.

Seth has never known who Argwings Khodek was, or why he got a street, but before the thought has finished forming itself into a question, one of those disrespectful courier motorcyclists, with the metal box welded to the space behind his buttocks, chooses that moment to veer dangerously close to the side-mirror of Seth's car as he edges past. Seth is distressed, and hisses sharply. For that one yawning second he is very angry. The courier is a fast millimetre away from vehicular desecration, and further, he is guilty of overtaking on the left. That is the problem with this country, Seth says to himself; no discipline at all.

***

His niece had come to speak to him after being thrown out of her house. Anastasia had always been a somewhat unserious personality, lacking in gravity and moral platform.

—Uncle, my mother is not feeling so well, she had said, she is not feeling well in herself.

—What is it? he had asked, thinking perhaps it was his sister's old knee trouble flaring up again.

Internally Misplaced

—No, it is—it is only her thoughts, Anastasia had replied, looking with concentration at the floor.

—What thoughts? Seth had asked. What thoughts are these that can make a person sick? What is she thinking of? How can thoughts make her sick?

This had been two months ago. Seth now knows that thoughts could make a person sick, because his own have had him retching every day for weeks. But he only throws up in the mornings and this has strangely made him feel much worse. This is a woman's rhythm. The mornings are the only time that he allows himself to feel cold panic, fear burning in his throat; his very ankles trembling. As soon as he finishes his morning preparation routine of putting on his uniform, he feels better. In his uniform he is soothed and symmetrical.

But at that time, at the time that Wacera had come to see him, he had not yet understood. He had asked her what her mother had been thinking about, to make herself sick in this way. This was the point at which his niece had been struck dumb yet curiously restless, and could only frown sorrowfully at her shoes. They had been green-coloured sandals, with a buckle on the side, and she had been shifting her foot from side to side as if admiring the silver square, as if trying to make the metal catch the light.

—No, it is — it is not that — it is not like that, she had murmured defensively to her feet.

—What is it, then? What are you trying to say?

It had taken him some time to winkle the problem out of the hole into which she had dug it. He had had to carefully tease it out of her, each strand of allusion and query spun thin and fragile, stretched to near-transparency. It had not been easy. He had advanced and she had retreated; when he had moved to the right, she had feinted left. He had shadow-boxed a question and she had deftly verbally ducked, all the while twisting her head sideways, placing her cheek on her shoulder, looking off to her side, like a wilted plant in a stiff breeze. Thrust, parry, thrust, deflect. Feint, dip, dodge, hedge, and then a tricky counterfeit: both Seth and his niece spoke Kikuyu with some skill. Her obliquely angled silhouette, turning and twisting away and then towards him, made her voice harder to understand, as if the wind whipping her body had snatched away her voice, as well. She had been trying to twist her torso into an even smaller target than her words.

***

Internally Misplaced

In the end, it emerged that the man who had unpeeled Anastasia Wacera's virginity from her, removed it like a banana skin, had subsequently moved on to juicier fruits. She was called Anastasia when working but Wacera when she was being herself, or at home with the family. The man had been her employer, so she had lost her job as well. Her mother had told her to go away, to get out of her house and find someone else to keep her and her shameful, pulsing womb. She had said she did not want mitumba women in her house. No soiled second-hand goods under her roof: which was similar to what Anastasia's erstwhile employer had told her, as well, except that he had been less polite.

In any case, people like Anastasia's former employer went for fruit salads of the more exotic kind; they mixed bits of orange with slices of banana drenched in foreign drinks all at once, mixed them up promiscuously like that and then served them in little glass bowls. Seth had watched Joshua the cook make fruit salad uncountable times for Madam, Madam's Husband and their guests. But they only ate fruit salad after the main course. They only ate this after the real food, after the stomach-fillers had been consumed. Unless, of course, the fruit salad was for breakfast; then they ate it by itself.

After her rage had subsided, Anastasia's mother, Seth's sister, had called Seth to ask him to do something about the situation.

—You work for them, she said. Do something — talk to that man. Talk to him for us; you speak their language.

Seth had had to explain that this was impossible because Wacera's ex-boss, her sometime-lover, and the owner of her now-swelling waist, was the husband of Madam's friend. He was also a business colleague of Madam's Husband, and almost as rich as Madam's Husband himself.

Worse, he was a Meru, with a temper to match.

It was rumoured that he had once cut off a rival's head and kept it in a basket, in his garage. The story went that after three weeks had passed, he had woken up early one morning and taken the basket to the police chief's house, where over some coffee, fried eggs, arrowroots and stewed tomatoes, and an undisclosed amount of money, the crime had been attributed to a mysterious sect, and had attracted only a small paragraph in the national press.

Seth's sister had nevertheless insisted that he should use his privileged position in Madam's house to intercede, to trade on his long record of loyal service.

Internally Misplaced

He had not tried to explain, and she would not have understood, that he felt he was about to need, for other purposes, all the credit with Madam he had. If he was not mistaken about this morning's events, he wanted his credit with Madam to be full to the brim and overflowing.

Seth had felt very disappointed at Wacera's thoughtlessness in getting pregnant, at her lack of foresight. In addition to everything else, Wacera had been earmarked for a potential respectable marriage to the young gardener at Madam's house, one Samuel Njogu, and they had been on the verge of announcing their engagement. This would have kept the good jobs in Seth's family, and also added to the numbers of Seth's family on the spacious grounds of Madam's house. Why would Wacera be so careless as to let herself be robbed of her future like that? Lack of professionalism, that is the problem, Seth thinks; lack of professionalism and dangerous inattention.

***

Seth is a good driver, he knows. He is always ready at his station by the cars at seven o'clock every morning. All three of them, both of Madam's cars and Seth, are well-presented and gleaming, and he stays on call every day until midnight. He has perfected the art of waiting in garages and courtyards and parking lots, on lawns and behind kitchens and outside the gates. He knows kiosk owners from Runda to Karen to Ruiru, and all points in between. He has seen all of Nairobi's mansions and eaten their food, delicate party-fare smuggled outside by compliant housegirls, thimbleful of fine spirits for the alcohol-inclined, although drivers were a non-drinking lot, as a whole.

They made up for it by smoking copiously, feverishly, each hurried lungful anticipating being unfinished. They had to be in the car and ready to go at any time, to have previously reconnoitered the parking situation for instant extraction. It required a fine touch, being a personal driver. You had to know at what time Madam's goodbye meant really goodbye and not let's stand around outside and talk for another twenty minutes, for no reason at all. This was just a skill you had to pick up, a job requirement, knowing when all those farewells finally meant business, when Madam meant:

—Let's go, get us out of here; this woman is driving me crazy with her pointless chatter: put the windows up and let's go.

His salary went up every year, like clock-work,

every year a decent raise, one new suit, and sometimes an additional hand-me down from Madam's husband, and a pair of good black shoes. He would be fine if everything carried on as expected. That was the problem, that and traffic. Seth did not know any more what to expect, what things were supposed to carry on as normal.

***

Seth had never been this close to death before, not death that mattered so much, so completely, death which changed everybody's life, without it mattering in the least who, exactly, had died.

As he passes the exit from Yaya Centre, Seth pauses to let a car join his lane, and recognises the blue Jaguar as belonging to one of Madam's friends. Madam's friend's husband has been dead for three years now: Seth is proud that after his unexpected demise, Madam had persuaded Madam's Husband to manage the finances of her friend. With all the businesses having had to close and the properties auctioned off, Madam's friend had been rescued in the nick of time by Madam's Husband. Still, proof of Madam's friend's bereavement, and her ensuing diminished means, could be found in the fact that Madam's friend was now forced to drive her own car herself. Another good job lost, thinks Seth—he had known her driver, now unemployed. Although Madam's Husband habitually frightens Seth mute, Madam's Husband's unyielding certainty is certainly a source of comfort to everybody around him, although not so much these days to Madam herself, a worrying development.

When Madam's Husband had suggested to the air this morning that Seth, and not Jackson, run this errand, Seth had not even thought to question why. Madam herself had been nowhere in sight, and Seth's deeply inscribed terror of Madam's Husband had taken over his body and manoeuvred him like a puppet on a string. Seth had heard, as if from far away, his own voice saying an instant Yes Sir as Madam's Husband's voice began its soft whispering, and then another Yes Sir when the whispering stopped.

Seth slows down and stays back a respectfully courteous but precise three feet away from the bumper of Madam's friend's car, a cautious foot hovering over his brake pedal. He does not trust women drivers, not even Madam's friends. The brakes are working well, but the car still needs to go in for service very urgently. That Madam's car's regular servicing is now two weeks overdue, Seth is well aware, but he cannot book an appointment for the job while the missing mechanic is still absent. Fear of the discovery that would be caused by the sudden eruption of payments to D.T. Dobie from Madam has begun to grow panicked green shoots in Seth's heart. He feels one such tendril uncurling now, and stretching, as if reaching for the sun.

—I'll see you then, in January, Ezekiel, the mechanic had said. He had been wiping his hands on dirty piece of cloth as he spoke. His overalls were clean and ironed.

—There's a slot free on the fifth, at ten. Do you want to bring it in then? Seth had agreed that the fifth looked like a likely date, and they had said goodbye. That was the last Seth had seen of him.

Once, fetching the car from servicing at closing time some months ago, and with an hour to kill before Madam's earliest next summons, Seth had given Ezekiel a lift home in Madam's car. He had been feeling generous, and Ezekiel had not only done an excellent service job as usual, but had also ingeniously crafted some extremely plausible additions to their longstanding private arrangement. Just before they had reached the turn-off beyond which the laneways in Ezekiel's neighbourhood became too rutted, too narrow-dirty to be for Madam's car, they had slowed to greet Ezekiel's wife, Amasabeth, who had been out on an errand to the kiosk. She had been holding a small bunch of onions in her hand, two candles, three tomatoes and a box of matches.

—This is mama-mtoto, Ezekiel had said, and to his wife: —Amasabeth, greet our visitor. He is one of my best clients. He is in charge of transportation for Mrs. Margaret Dorobo.

Seth had declined to stay for tea that day, but he had promised to one day come for a proper visit, on one of his days off. When Madam was next away, he would be back for a meal and a talk. He had waved goodbye and driven off, and had never been back again. And now Ezekiel is missing.

Seth nudges at this thought like a tongue worrying a swollen gum. He has been trying to call Ezekiel on his cell-phone for two weeks now. He had first called on the fourth, wanting to suggest that they postpone the tentatively scheduled maintenance service for the fifth until things had cooled down a bit. There had been no answer. Seth had called a few more times, increasingly anxious. Madam had already asked him twice if it is was not yet time to take the car in, but that had been in December, before the other things had happened. She has not asked him since, but even so, Seth could not forever count on her strange mood making her forgetful. Finally, he had made a call to D.T. Dobie's customer service desk, pretending to be somebody else's driver who wanted to reach Ezekiel. The first time he had called, there had been no answer. Seth had not known whether Dobie were back at work then—some companies were still closed, even after all this time.

He had called again and this time a voice, with none of the dispassion normally displayed by corporate receptionists, had told him that they were very worried about Ezekiel as he was one of their best mechanics, and nobody had seen him since he had gone off to Nyanza for the holidays. Ezekiel had spoken to one of his colleagues from Kisumu town, so they knew he had definitely made it there, but since then nobody has heard of him at all. They cannot trace his wife, or his relatives, or his neighbours here in Kibera, and of course even in Nairobi it has been difficult to know anything with certainty at all. There is no news: he is just missing.

Seth values his soul's record-book in heaven, where he is sure that the accounts are rigorous but above-board: he is not a thief. The D.T. Dobie invoices he delivers to Madam, complete with the company's logo, are for the amount of the standard Dobie rates; sometimes even below. It is only that the mechanic, Ezekiel,—who, let it be strictly noted, is after all employed at Dobie: this is a virtuous fact– has a duplicate invoice and receipt book, and Madam likes to pay in cash, which in this instance, is serendipitous. Madam gives him the brown manila envelope with cash in them, and he conscientiously returns to her the change and the receipts for the exact amounts.

Her domestic filing systems consist of neatly-stacked up and labelled cardboard boxes, full of brown manila envelopes. Madam, extracting the change and writing the amount on the front, puts this envelope and its associated invoices and receipts away in its appropriate box. Seth thinks that Madam uses these envelopes because she wants to categorise and store the essence of all the hands that touched them and all the relationships involved, perhaps for examination at another time.

The frugal beauty and simple seriousness of this arrangement appeals to Seth.

As long as Madam intends to pay a certain sum for certain services however, Seth sees no harm in combining his own interests with those of her well-maintained machine, for which he feels a strong sibling affection. He and the car are good allies, a good teaming up of well-oiled German parts and limbs, of fossil fuel and flesh.

With the amount of Madam's money that has been creatively adapted to new uses with Ezekiel's help, Seth has even managed, over the years, to afford small luxuries. He has a Nokia cell phone and has in fact just migrated to Safaricom's Jambo tariff. This has allowed him and his sister to discuss Wacera's fate in the odd moments when neither one of them is working, as for a reasonable amount of money and provided he keeps his conversations short, Seth can now afford to make phone calls at any time of the day or night, which is useful, especially with things being what they are these days.

***

The traffic finally starts to creep through the Hurlingham shopping centre. Further along, the walls of the Department of Defense barracks rise up, grey and grave, and begin their protective march alongside the rows of traffic. These walls are one of the only sizeable exterior vertical public surfaces in Nairobi which do not wear bedraggled garlands of last December's campaign posters, already now tattered and torn. Seth finds this reassuring. The lines of the wall's cement-blocks seem attentive, alert. It is clear to Seth that the wall itself is ready to defend this country with its stern, rough, concrete texture.

There is a line at the Barclay's ATM, across the way, at the Hurlingham Barclays Bank. The line stretches almost to the low retaining wall, against which a fat woman in a yellow boubou is leaning. She is so large that the voluminous garment only smooths over, but cannot blend, her prodigious bulging outline. She is sweating profusely in the sun, and the loose end of her headwrap is listing forlornly alongside her over-permed hair. Seth fancies that the blue Barclay's eagle is looking somewhat tense these days, as if it knows that its mechanised agents are not up to the job of dispensing enough cash to satisfy fear; they cannot calm hysteria. Their creativity stops at the ability to swallow disobedient debit cards, or delinquent ones. Those, the ATMs can battle: anything else is not on their job description.

In the next lane, a bicyclist suddenly swerves onto the hustling matatu's path, then wobbles away, weaves wildly, and finally falls. The cyclist is on his back in the road, looking dazed. His shoes have come off. He had been carrying some papers. They are scattered all over the road, crumpling and flattening under speeding tyres. A small gash is bleeding in the cyclist's head, over one of his eyes. The matatu has driven on. Seth sees a small tattered boy steal the cyclist's shoes and run away. A half-hearted crowd begins to gather, not so much to help the cyclist as to observe his fate. Nairobi is always ready for a spectacle, no matter how banal its ingredients—people will always gather for a free feast for their eyes.

At the Barclays, there is a commotion at the front of the line. A man is shouting angrily, his arms jerking though the air. Another man in a badly dry-cleaned black suit and carrying a battered leather briefcase looks at his watch, shakes his head in disgust and then, after an upward glance at the sun, strides around the corner to the bank itself. Next, a young woman in jeans steps out of line and, extracting her cell phone from her beaded bag, dials a number and starts to talk with an urgent tilt to her head. The line continues to fragment, one discrete person at a time. After watching three different people walk up to the computerised screen, punch a button, and then turn away in disgust, Seth deduces that the ATM has closed itself down, probably because it has run out of cash. The Barclays eagle definitely looks worried, Seth thinks, and snorts sardonically at himself, automatically slowing down as the brake lights in front of him gleam red. The vigilantly professional part of him has noticed that it is time to make a decision about what to do after Argwings Khodek. State House road will be jammed as usual, should he try to give Valley Road a chance? The problem is that this will bring him, or rather it will bring Madam's car, too near Uhuru Park, and Seth on principle always steers clear of places which threaten Madam's car. State House it is. As he turns left to go to Dennis Pritt and then State House road, Seth notices as he shift gears that there is a slight stickiness, a faint hitch, to the clutch.

Where is Ezekiel?

***

State House road is a comforting stretch of tarmac, especially from the point of view of a professional driver. It is true that Bishop's road has a sign that proclaims it the safest street in Nairobi, but faced with a choice between trusting in Israeli Embassy security and the security arrangements of the republic's president, Seth sees no choice at all. Israelis die all the time, as CNN has repeatedly shown, but no Kenyan president has ever been assassinated, and that is a fact. Terrorists always want to kill the Jews, but why would they turn their attention to Kikuyu gentlemen? Although, with these new things happening these days, who knows. Madam's friend had said, not ten days ago, that she had cancelled her holiday planned for the Coast. Seth had been driving Madam and her friends back to their homes after a function. Madam had said to her friend, then, that she would not let fear dictate her actions, but, of course, that had been before everything else had happened. Besides, Seth argues eloquently to himself, do you mean to tell me that if Al Qaeda can bomb America, they will be defeated by Israelis here in Nairobi? Al Qaeda obviously has no quarrel with the Kenyan president. Seth, taking in State House's lawns, feels his head nod thrice, to agree.

Along this stretch of road, security and safety are a certainty, and a minimum decorum amongst drivers is expected. This certainty and decorum, of course, is only for some people; it can be quite bad for others. For example, Seth has heard about a person who had lost control of his car, right alongside State House, and inadvertently crashed into the presidential wall. It was rumoured that he had been drunk, but perhaps not Luo, and after the State House guards had shot him, the autopsy report had been lost. Even the car had been confiscated, as part of 'the evidence.' It was impossible to know if all this had happened because the unfortunate and possibly drunk man had been a compatriot from the lakeside region.

Despite himself, a hot, anonymous rage fills Seth.

—Burning and murdering and what have you, he thinks disjointedly. Running around with pangas like as if they think blood can be replaced in a body: as if people are like cars and have spare-tyre lives which they will use the next morning after their deaths. You can't just stop in the middle of having your throat cut, and, using some handy tools, just exchange your life for one with no puncture and better treads He has been told that socialism is able to excite and degrade the brain in this fashion. When Seth's friend Mwangi had told him about the driver who crashed into State House, he had added an editorial comment at the end.

—They can't even drive a car, much less anything else! Mwangi had said, clicking his tongue in disgust.

As he swings by the windows of State House Girls', Seth reviews again his own job performance, to check himself for fault and to marshal his thoughts in his mind in case Madam or Madam's Husband asks him to account for himself, which he is no longer sure he can do. Seth likes his place in the world, but its edges are getting fuzzy, dissolving away, and the more fragile it gets, the more he anxious he becomes, and the more appreciative of what is threatened by an unseen and ominous fugue.

The thing is about these athungus, and he means this not in the literal sense of "white people" but more neutrally of "rich employer": the thing is that if you play your cards right you become necessary for them, like a daily cup of tea. They forget how to drive and become afraid of traffic at night and before they know it, they cannot go anywhere without you.

He slows down for the left turn into Arboretum Drive, whose leafy shelter soothes almost as much as thoughts of Madam usually do. Madam only goes abroad once a year these days, if even that, and she mostly requires visits to hairdressers, weddings, charity events and her friends' houses. She does all the shopping herself though, she knows the prices of things, Madame does, she knows where all the shillings and cents in her house go, she has a grasp on things.

Seth is now behind a large Land Rover Discovery with red license plates. Seth has professional opinions on these machines: they are the only things he gets argumentative about. He has a small but surprisingly comprehensive collection of car manuals and car magazines The American four by fours are certainly roomy, he'll give you that. Some people are now using them more than the Mercedes. That, and having bodyguards, seems to be the new trend. Maybe because American cars encourage American behaviour? Seth thinks about this, about the various types of cars that Madam and Madam's husband's friends and business acquaintances drive. Yes, the American cars are encouraging strange behaviour. Although of course they are very nice and big, with all that fancy chrome and roll bars and extra lights.

If you drove the car of an important person or an important person's wife, the cars were guaranteed to be excellent, and to be of several German makes also, that or British, but definitely one or the other. German, and solid, or British and somewhat flashy and ponderous, but of course, as Seth knows, the Japanese or was it the Chinese have now taken over some of the British. The German four-wheel drive by Mercedes is a mistake, Seth thinks, it simply looks like a box of matches on wheels. He thinks the toy cars he used to play with in Mathare were like that, ugly angles and liable to overturn at any moment.

Seth's car magazines were always somewhat delayed, because he could only buy them from one special stall, and Madam's routes did not take him there often. They were second-hand, of course, the magazines, but still enough to keep him able to hold his own with other drivers when the need arose. The other drivers were often men like him, long-term employees with solid reputations. No beeping or honking, except when requested to do so. Just beep and let her know we are here, Madam will sometimes say, and he will beep. But at the gates of stranger's homes he does not beep unless told to by Madam; he flashes the headlights instead. If the watchman is even half-way decent at his job no noise is necessary at all, the gates will open and the car will glide silently on, as is right and proper.

One of Madam's friends' husbands had just purchased an Italian for himself. A Maserati; but he wouldn't let the driver drive the car for him, so what was the use of that? It was a nice car, no doubt about that, but drivers needed work. Seth has no use for the driverless rich, he finds them selfish, especially these young ones, who were buying their own cars now but not hiring drivers. Madam's Husband had a Hummer, which of course Jackson drove – he had had the first one in Nairobi. Seth had been allowed to sit in it, once, when the household was asleep and he had given Jackson a whole packet of Sportsman cigarettes. Even

Jackson had been impressed enough to show off.

Seth strongly disapproves of the new trend towards flying that the Nairobi rich have been exhibiting. Aeroplanes are nice, but what do you do for transport on the other side? Of course Seth flies where Margaret does, if it is in Kenya. She simply pays for him to accompany her, so she can have a driver when she lands. Except of course if it is a game drive: those are a completely different type of driver, more adventurous, but less well-paid, of course. They are paid to be slightly dashing, somewhat world-weary, dangerous even, they have to excite white tourists while delivering their practiced lectures. Seth has a professional regard but also a slight contempt for these drivers, they are good at what they do, admittedly, but why do it at all?

At a recent party by one of Madam's husband's friends, the drivers had gathered to ridicule one of their own, Muriuki, Winston, or William or something like that, who had been so stupid as to get drunk at a party his employers were attending. It is quite easy if you know the housegirls to get a bottle of whisky at a time like this, and Muriuki had been found snoring and drunk at the wheel of his car. They had fired him and left him there, dead drunk outside their friend's gate. Seth knew he would hear of Muriuki again soon enough.

Somebody's gardener will have spoken to somebody else's maid who will know the brother of somebody's watchman, and Muriuki will have been found again, in greatly diminished circumstances, of course. Now reduced to being just a watchman, on endless night shifts, walking about muffled in old hats and rags and with scarves around your head and big heavy coats, and no doubt a rung'u or some other thing to lug around. Nairobi is really quite small like that, in the end.

But these days, Madam isn't talking at all, isn't saying anything except for things like "We're going to town, that Italian place." And then she doesn't say anything else, expects Seth to know what Italian place she means as she sits in the back, silenced by grief and loss and pain so big it is heavy, like another passenger, or a body in the trunk. Or she says "Home, please." and goes back inside her pain, closing the door behind her, leaving her solitary, trapped in her mourning with all the curtains closed. Her cell phone rings and remains unanswered. This is not Madam-type behaviour at all.

Seth has on more than one occasion turned his head to hear her response and been met with nothing, just her eyes which are on nothing at all. He took the wrong turn once, on purpose, just to test her, to see if she was still aware that she was in a moving car with another human being driving it: and that time too, there was nothing in her eyes.

The only one Madam seems to see at all these days is Madam's Husband. Madam has gathered all her seeing, every last bit, and pointed it all in one direction. She has started looking at Madam's Husband, really looking, as if her eyes were a surgeon's knife and he a disease, staring and staring at him in silence. Madam's husband doesn't even notice. Or he notices but he doesn't care. It is just a look, what can it do, what can it possibly understand of your life, your world, your dealings and decisions?

***

The shelter of the trees of the arboretum ends, and Seth drives smoothly up the hill to Riverside. At the top of the hill, at the junction of Ring Road Riverside and Riverside proper, there is a policeman lounging by the curb. The policeman is not directing traffic, he is not checking cars. He is wearing the police uniform as if it belongs to someone else, as if he had that morning woken up naked and disoriented in strange surroundings, with nothing but this set of police clothes to put on.

The peach walls of the Australian High Commission and the hedges of Chiromo campus pull Seth out of his reverie. He merges onto Waiyaki way, pausing only to give way to a lorry full of men in green riot gear and red berets, and accelerates up to the appropriate speed, feeling the smooth pick-up of the car with satisfaction. He loves driving this car—he cannot think of being parted from it; he and this car belong together. The angular bell-tower of Consolata catches his eye for an instant; the UNHCR headquarters flashes past.

As the cars sweep up towards Westlands, another matatu with "Da PERFUMED garden" with the 'perfume' done in dripping green and purple font charges past on the right, cuts in front of Seth, and swerves into the far left lane. The lorry with the men in red berets is just in front of it, and the matatu driver swings back out onto the center lane, as if to overtake it. The lorry, at this same instant, swings out to its right also, towards the matatu, and the matatu swerves wildly away and hits the blue Pajero in the far right lane. All lanes come to a stop, as the lorry full of the men in red berets has skewed across the lanes, like a drunken crane, and halted.

As soon as the lorry has stopped, the men at the

back start to disembark, swinging down from the rope at the back onto the ground, where their boots make a hollow 'thunk' sound as they land. They are all armed. Their faces are grim, and as each new man hits the ground, the air seems to harden. The driver of the Pajero has climbed out of his car and is inspecting the damage, but also glancing towards the men with a wary eye. The passengers in the matatu are sitting still, held to their seats as if glued there. No one makes a sound. Two of the men in the red berets go round the front to the matatu driver's side, and, jerking the door open, pull him out of the van. He staggers down.

The birds are still.

Salvation arrives.

A long loud honk from the back, a deep throaty trumpet of a sound. It is like releasing a fart into a hostage situation —from someone in a car far enough behind not to have seen the men in green and red, comes a repeated exasperated hooting that is joined in chorus by two or three others. Something snaps back into place, reality shimmers and recognises itself. The lorry's driver hops into the cab and, starting the engine, pulls it off to the side. Seth, or the part of him that still knows how to drive, eases into the empty space, past the confused cluster of men and cars, drives up to the roundabout, swings right, and is decanted into the immediately comforting embrace of Westlands' disarray.

***

Hawkers are ranging the center strip, selling an assortment of goods catering to the mysterious combinations of Nairobi's needs. Here for sale are DVDs, magazines, flags, small sculptures of cars done in twisted metal, roses in red, orange, white, and other flowers, Arsenal paraphernalia and Manchester United t-shirts, strawberry-flavoured car air fresheners, and puppies. Seth is taken by surprise by a wave of emotion that sweeps over him, which he recognises as nostalgia for all that is right in front of his eyes. For the solid white-and-blue bulk of the Sarit Centre. For the curio sellers on the other side of the roundabout working in cartels to sell their carvings, for the old Uchumi with the faded red paint back there, where Madam used to do all her shopping before the Nakumatt Supermarkets hit town.

He glides down lower Kabete Road and, at the furniture maker's, swings smoothly into the familiar welcoming right turn. This will be the last place in Nairobi to burn. He has an official right to be here, to drive the roads in these safe and leafy enclaves of calm. There is a girl handing out leaflets for a new restaurant. Can someone still be thinking of starting a new business, isn't everyone who is able to moving their money abroad as fast as possible and arranging for visas and exit plans? Soon, only those who have nowhere else to go will be left behind.

The country has been on the move quite a lot these past few weeks, all things considered. Everybody first did the annual migration home for the holidays, then re-arranged themselves around their polling station. Then, after everything began, people also moved their lives indoors, hunkering down in living rooms and inner courtyards behind their gates, like turtles in the sun with a hawk in the sky. Circles closing in on smaller circles, compressing them, inexorably deepening the fear that lies on the floor like a thick pool of dirty oil. Everyone inside, heads down, eyes tightly closed, lips moving in prayer.

***

As he drives past the well-tended hedges, and self-consciously beautiful outer gardens, Seth waits for the liquid contentment that usually slides down the back of his throat at this point on the drive home to find him.

Internally Misplaced

It does not come. In its place is something else—a distinct and growing tension. His shoulders stiffen. Jackson is inside the gates—he is inside the protective perimeter of Madam's house.

Seth can almost hear the thing he fears. He can hear it growling in the German engine below him. Seth has seen it on CNN at Madam's house, this thing. A malevolent child, creating strangely heaped multi-car sculptures around lamp-posts and rippling bridges into skirts. He knows what it can do: it is a mad artisanal monster with a taste for blood. Heaving in a breath, Seth tries to calls on a courage that has changed address and will not answer.

Seth had looked inside the large box before he had put it in the boot. Madam's Husband had told him that morning—had whispered it into the air as if commanding ghosts—to, upon paying for them, count them when he had them in his hands, and Seth had counted. There were two hundred and thirty-five. Two hundred and thirty-five silver-sharp edges waiting in the light. The light brown wood of the panga handles had looked incongruous, innocent, as if the pale smooth planes were new to the world.

A trickle of moisture runs into Seth's eye and stings. He blinks; he had not noticed he was sweating, and he fumbles for a handkerchief and wipes his brow. When Madam's Husband called him this morning, Seth had thought it was because Madam's Husband needed Jackson to take him to his regular golf game at the Muthaiga club, and indeed, Madam's Husband had gone off with Jackson and his golf clubs much as usual, after having given Seth his instructions about the box in the boot.

Seth rounds another of the endless curves snaking into what was once forest and sees a man with an orange shirt and two large Alsatians on a chain. The tails of the dogs are wagging fondly but the relationship between the man and the dogs is not right. He does not own the dogs, Seth can tell, he is not the one they adore. He is simply exercising them. He is obviously familiar to them, and they will obey him, but only to a point.

He rubs his ear, which has started to itch, shuffles his bottom around on the leather seat and then wipes his upper lip. He reaches down to the radio knob and turning it on, begins to fiddle with the dial. He flicks through the stations, disembodied voices, snatches of song, an advertising jingle for a cooking fat and then static again. He switches the knob off and then on again.

46

Internally Misplaced

Here is the clock at Red Hill. He is nearly there. He pauses at the intersection and listens to himself breathe. The fuel tank is full. He has five hundred shillings on him because of some change he has not yet had a chance to return to Madam. His driving license is in order, and so is his I.D. The grass outside his window is an almost painful deep bright green. There is a different clock on each of the faces of the white cube-shaped head balancing on top of a slender pole. A risk. The clock is black and white. The longer of the two hands moves. Just an edge, a twitch; Seth is barely sure he has seen it but it was pointing at twenty-nine past just a second ago and now it is pointing at thirty, straight up and down.

The car stalls, and Seth jumps. The Mercedes never stalls. It is not that kind of car. Seth's hand reaches down and turns the ignition to the 'off' switch, and waits a beat. He wipes his palms on his trouser legs. He reaches up again and grips the steering wheel position firmly in the correct ten-minutes-to-two o'clock position, turns the ignition switch on and turns the car gently, smoothly homewards. He greets the guards at the gates as always, with a friendly wave of his hand and a smile. Seth and the guards sometimes make jokes about having to walk two kilometres to the kiosk to get a pack of mozos when at work, when where they live there is always a kiosk a few paces away.

It is then that the thought occurs to him. He realises, as if he has just been attempting to sit down on something sharp, that some of those kiosks in those places where the guards are from are gone now, they have floated away in spires of smoke, surrounded by sparks of angry orange and leaping red flames.

Perhaps the distance between kiosks has been equalised: a long walk either way. Seth himself lives in the row behind Madam's house, in the shelter of a white-washed one-roomed haven of sanity furnished by mended bits of furniture that Madam had, for her own well-judged reasons, decided to discard. Seth sees in his mind the wooden table with one metal leg that sits in the corner of his room. The table leg that is metal is a piece of tubing that Seth has bolted on. On top of the table is a stack of car magazines and a small black bible, shiny with use. Everything else is put away into the small drawer, or under the bed, because Seth is an orderly man who likes to keep his surfaces clean. He likes to see the tops of things looking properly dusted and wiped down, likes the symmetry of nothing but angles and corners and flat surfaces in sight.

***

Internally Misplaced

Seth glides into the driveway and halts at the gate, letting the murmur of the big car's engine signal the guard to open the gate. The guards and household staff can distinguish the precise rich contralto of Madam's Mercedes Benz from the more gritty one of her new four wheel-drive, can tell while the car is still at the nearest kiosk from Madam's house that Jackson and the Hummer are coming back.

Sometimes they can even tell the mood required for the upcoming arrivals: certain speeds of coming round the final curve and the sound of certain well-known bumps being negotiated in a different gear from normal, can be surprisingly explicit indications of the temperature of the owners of the house.

He drives into the parking lot, and into the garage. It is very quiet after the noise of the engine is cut off abruptly by Seth with one swift wrist-motion. Seth does not know if Madam even knows about the errand on which he had been sent by Madam's Husband. The brooding passion that has engulfed Madam has her so deeply in its grip that she seems to glow like the furnace room of a coal-driven train. She is a forge in which something new is being created. Her will is roiling and massing and Seth can no longer read her signs.

When Seth opens the back door of the house

and steps into the kitchen, he finds Joshua the cook chopping vegetables. The radio is switched on low, to some music radio station, but Joshua is not singing along under his breath as usual. Seth turns his head and sees Jackson seated at the kitchen table, silently reading a newspaper, his back straight and composed as always and his hands placed on the table on either side of the page. Seth steps towards him to ask him to tell Madam's Husband that he, Seth, has returned with Madam's Husband's box. It would be rude for Seth to go over Jackson's head and talk directly to Madam's Husband while Jackson is in the house. He will deliver his news to Madam's Husband in private, and in Kikuyu of course, at the appropriate time.

***

Joshua is still chopping vegetables. Jackson becomes aware of Seth's presence: there is a deepening of the stillness with which he holds his head. His hands move on the table, closer to the page. He lifts his eyes to look at Seth. Seth opens his mouth to speak, but Jackson stands up and turns to the corridor leading to the dining room and Madam's Husband's study. Seth follows him.

***

Other **Kwani** titles

Kwanini? Series

~Binyavanga Wainaina -*Discovering Home* (ISBN: 9966-7008-4-6)

~Binyavanga Wainaina -*Beyond River Yei* (ISBN: 9966-7008-7-0)

~Binyavanga Wainaina -*How To Write About Africa* (ISBN: 9966-7008-2-X)

~Yvonne Adhiambo Owour -*Weight of Whispers* (ISBN: 9966-7008-3-8)

~Chimamanda Adichie -*You In America* (ISBN: 9966-7008-0-3)

~Wambui Mwangi -*Internally Misplaced* (ISBN: 9966-7008-8-9)

~Richard Onyango -*The Life and Times of Richard Onyango*
  (ISBN: 9966-7008-5-4)

~Mzee Ondego –The Life of Mzee Ondego (ISBN: 9966-7182-0-6)

~CKW -*Kwanini Special Edtion* (ISBN: 9966-7008-1-1)